KiddiVersity's™
Cappy's Adventure Book Series

Cappy's ™
New York City Adventure

By
Toni F. O'Hanlon

Illustrated by
Stephanie Payne

KiddiVersity™
New York, NY

Printed in the United States of America by
KiddiVersity LLC
P.O. Box 8573
Pelham, New York 10803
Email: info@kiddiversity.com
www.kiddiversity.com

ISBN -13 978-1466370272
ISBN-10 1466370270

Library of Congress Catalog Card Number 2011918020

O'Hanlon, Toni F.
First published 2010
Cappy's New York City Adventure
Author: Toni O'Hanlon
Illustrated: Stephanie Payne
34 p.

Summary: Cappy the Caterpillar and his best friend Walter Finch are on yet another adventure! Entertaining preschoolers through humor and rhyme helping children to understand what happens around them, everyday in their neighborhood. This time, Cappy and Walter get the opportunity to visit a busy city. They experience the awe inspiring tall buildings along with the exciting hustle and bustle they encounter on the busy city streets!

1. Caterpillar – Juvenile Fiction 2. Animal and Human Characters – Juvenile Fiction 3. Sanitation Trucks – Juvenile Fiction

September 11, 2001
NYC
A DAY OF REMEMBRANCE

As a born and raised New Yorker, 9-11 strikes close to home
for me in more ways than one.
I stood, walked and did business with people who worked
in the towers on various occasions for many years.

Sometimes, it is difficult to find words that could
express such deep sorrow.

My heart goes out to the countless victims and their family's.

May God Bless all their souls.

May God Bless America.

Hi! My name is Cappy!
This is my best friend
Walter Finch.

Today we are going to visit
New York City.
Where the buildings are tall.

Where nothing, I said nothing!
Is tiny or small!

We get on the train
It chugs this way and that.

Soon we'll be there
In no time flat
and that will be that.

The city is buzzing
with people and cars.

No time to stop
to admire the stars!

The sidewalk is crowded

Everyone walks very fast.

Is this Times Square?
Someone had asked.

Let's wave for a cab

We cannot be late.

He'll get us there quick
we won't have to wait.

The Empire State Building is the tallest by far.

See the tippy top?
It's as high as a star!

Cappy, step in quick
before the elevator doors close!

WATCH OUT! WATCH OUT!
Look out for your toes!

UP, UP, WE GO!
Up, Up and away!

Now this is how
we like to spend the day!

We're off to see the top!
Hold on tight, with all our might!

We feel our
ears go 'pop'-'pop-pop'!!

Walter look down! Look down!
People look so small!

Everyone looks the same
size from here.
Even if they're 10 feet tall!

It's time to go.
We are done with play.
We're getting very tired.
Tomorrow is another day.

BUY CAPPY the Plush Toy NOW!!!

Hi! I am CAPPY!

Only $12.95

Go to - **www.kiddiversity.com**
to buy our plush toy or

Mail your order to:

KiddiVersity LLC, PO Box 8573 Pelham, NY 10803

NAME: _____

Address: _____

City: _____ State: _____ ZIP: _____

Email: _____

Telephone: _____ Quantity: _____

Price $12.95 plus $4.95 shipping & handling per unit
ENCLOSE CHECK OR MONEY ORDER PAYABLE TO KIDDIVERSITY LLC

Our plush toy meets and exceeds United States and International Health and Safety Standards.
All material used is hyper allergenic. No beans or beads.

Additional books written by this author:

"Cappy
the Caterpillar"

"Cappy's Firehouse
Adventure"

"Cappy's Police
Adventure"

"Cappy's Dr. Maloney
Adventure"

"Cappy's Garbage
Truck Adventure"

"Cappy's New York
City Adventure"

"Cappy's Playground
Adventure"

"Cappy's Farm
Adventure"

"Cappy's Schoolhouse
Adventure"

"Cappy's Dentist
Adventure"